Take a Hike, Miles and Spike!

Travis Foster and Ethan Long

chronicle books · san francisco

Take care,
GRIZZLY BEAR!

Stay loose, MOOSE!

Buh-bye,
BUTTERFLY!

Ta-ta for now, COW!
Cheerio, CROW!

Smell you soon, RACCOON!
Peace out, RAINBOW TROUT!

We're outta here, DEER!
Can't stay, BLUE JAY!

In a shake,
RATTLESNAKE!

Goodbye, DRAGONFLY!
Farewell, GAZELLE!
Gotta go, BUFFALO!

URRRRRRGH!

PANT PANT
PANT
PANT
PANT
DRIP DRIP
DRIP
DRIP

Clear the water, OTTER!

TAKE A
MILES

HIKE,
AND SPIKE!

We acted dumb,
chum.

Let's try again then.

Want to go, BUFFALO?

Let's head out,
RAINBOW TROUT!

Let's vamoose, MOOSE!
OK.

Join the fun,
EVERYONE!

Are we there yet, MARMOSET?
What's a MARMOSET?

The End
Ugh. I think I'm lost.